About the Author

Mark Leah has been married to his wife, Lindsey, for nearly thirty years and is a father of three and a grandfather of two. He was brought up in "Tinsle" (Tintwistle), within the Peak District, and has many fine memories of his childhood. These memories have been the inspiration for Mark's stories. Mark works as a Kinder/Edale National Trust ranger within the Peak District and has been involved in many conservation projects over his twenty-four years of service. Mark's time in this job has also inspired his writing and illustrations.

Tinsle Tales

Benniebee/Walliewasp

Mark Leah

Tinsle Tales

Benniebee/Walliewasp

Nightingale Books

A CIP catalogue record for this title is
available from the British Library.
ISBN 978-1-83875-380-1

Nightingale Books is an imprint of
Pegasus Elliot MacKenzie Publishers Ltd.
www.pegasuspublishers.com

First Published in 2021

Nightingale Books
Sheraton House Castle Park
Cambridge England

Printed & Bound in Great Britain

Dedication

For Red Rose

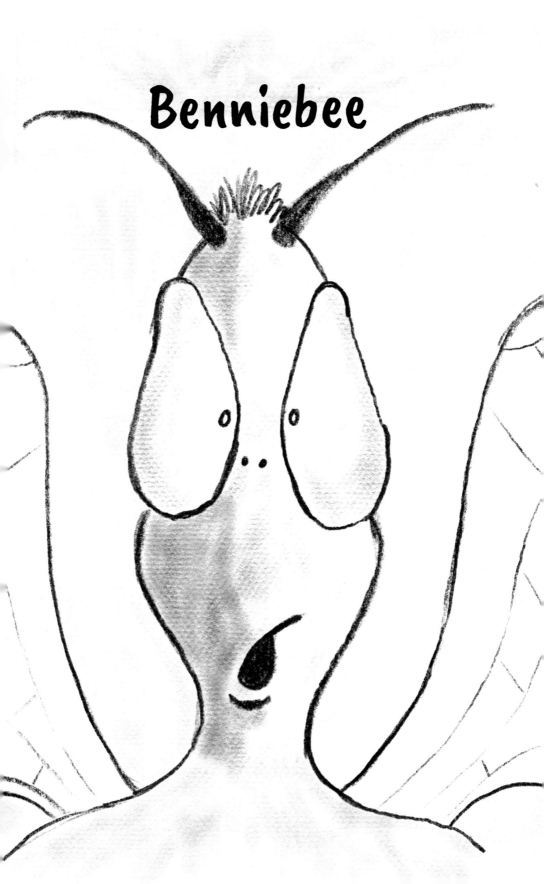

Benniebee

Benniebee was confused. He knew that he belonged somewhere, but where? All Benniebee could think about were the strange towers popping up everywhere.

The closer Benniebee got to the strange towers, with their long, grey flowers, the more Benniebee's antenna dipped. So, with what little spirit Benniebee had left, he decided to leave this strange place and headed in the opposite direction.

Benniebee felt better further away from the strange tower with its long, grey flowers and, before long, he noticed his buzz getting louder. Then, all of a sudden, it happened. A word popped into his head.

As Benniebee passed the large puddle with a funny name, he heard something not too far away. It was something that sounded similar to his buzz but slightly different. Deep within his heart, a voice was telling him to follow the sound.

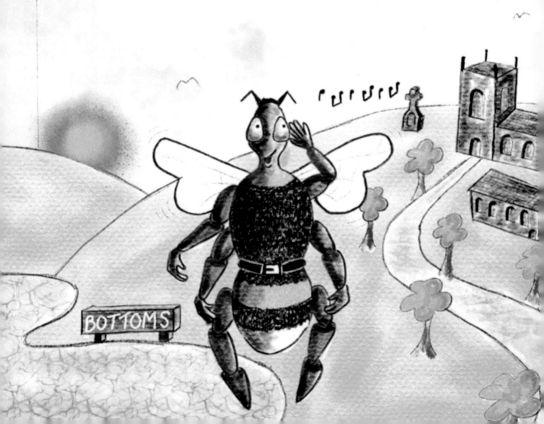

Benniebee continued to listen to what his heart was telling him and before too long he was hovering next to an unusually large stone. The sound seemed to be coming from behind the stone. Also, he noticed hanging around him what looked like butterflies holding hands.

After leaving the curious, large stone and butterflies that appeared to dance along to the music, it happened again. Another word popped into Benniebee's increasingly clearing head.

All of a sudden, Benniebee realised he was in the queendom of Tinsle. He knew this because his heart told him so. As he bumbled his way down the lane, he came across a field of daisies and he instinctively knew what to do.

With the sweet taste of nectar still lingering on Benniebee's tongue, he doubled his efforts and flapped his wings even harder, which was made easier because of the sticky liquid he had just eaten.

Benniebee's antenna began twitching once again, and then it happened for a third time. Another word formed in his progressively liberated noggin.

Now that Benniebee's sophisticated sensory system was beginning to break free from the effects of the strange tower with its long, grey flowers, he remembered a different type of insect which had stuck up for bees a long time ago, and an image floated into his head.

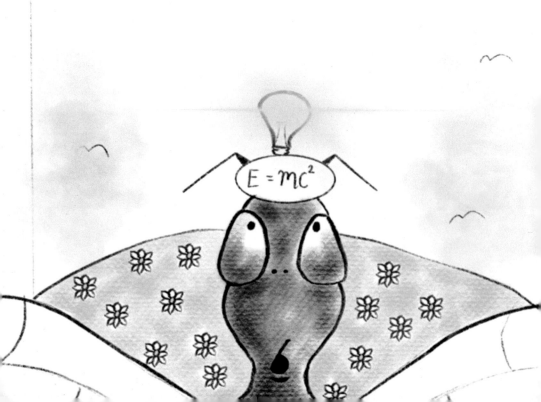

Benniebee started to feel that he was getting closer to home. His antenna was beginning to straighten out and he had an incredible feeling of peace, which swept through his entire exoskeleton.

It was when Benniebee moved quickly around the forget-me-not flowers growing on both sides of the beautifully maintained garden path that his eyes took in a scene of beauty standing on a pearl white step of the lodge. It was this that made his heart skip a beat.

Standing on the pearl white step of the lodge, which bore the name Bee Kind Cottage, stood Benniebee's wife and family waiting with open arms. This was when Benniebee's eyes moistened with loving tears of joy, for he knew he was home.

Walliewasp

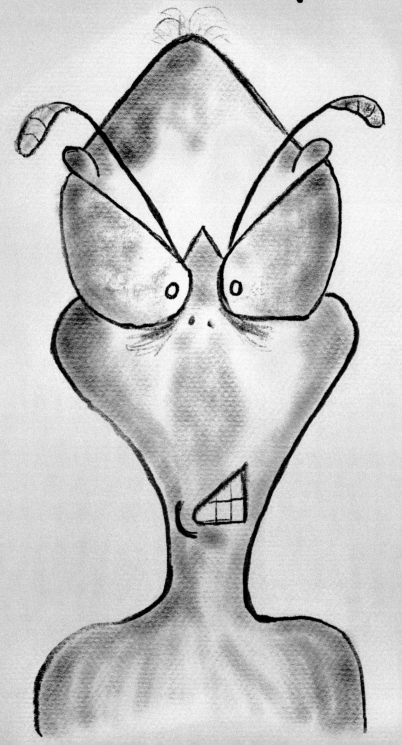

Walliewasp was a resident of the Queendom of Tinsle. He was a quick-tempered little insect but there was a reason for this.

Newsagents

Can you imagine that whenever you fly past one of the strange-looking insects, all they want to do is swat at you?

Every time Walliewasp was swatted, he developed a greater lack of understanding for the strange-looking insects.

One of the things that could lift Walliewasp's mood was the many fallen apples that lie beneath the trees in the late summer.

And this was where Walliewasp was heading. This particular tree was one of Walliewasp's favourites. Nevertheless, getting there was full of danger.

This special, mystical tree was situated in the middle of Swallows Wood, which was located on the far edge of the Queendom of Tinsle.

On his quest, Walliewasp had to pass through an odd-looking garden made of glass cylinders which each held a yellow nectar.

This place was of interest to Walliewasp and he settled on one of the cylinders. He was about to take a sip from the glass when, out of nowhere, swat!

Walliewasp was startled and he could feel his temper rising. All he wanted to do was try the bright coloured liquid.

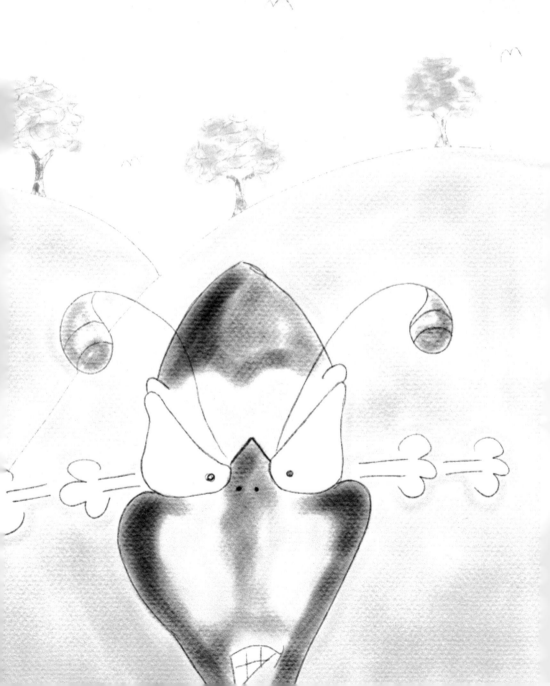

With his head throbbing, he turned his attention back to the mystical tree and focused on the crusade ahead of him.

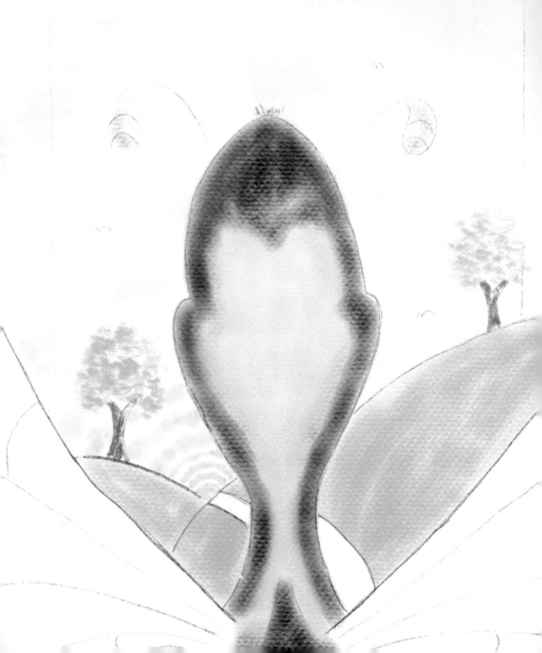

The courageous Walliewasp had survived the perplexing garden and understood that there would be additional risks on his journey to the mystical tree.

Walliewasp found himself flying down a lane which was covered by oak, rowan and silver birch trees. At the end of the lane, it split into two different directions.

CROSSGATE LANE

Now, Walliewasp knew that if he were to take the left fork of the lane it would be quicker than if he were to take the right fork.

However, even though it was quicker to go left, he knew that it was a more dangerous route.

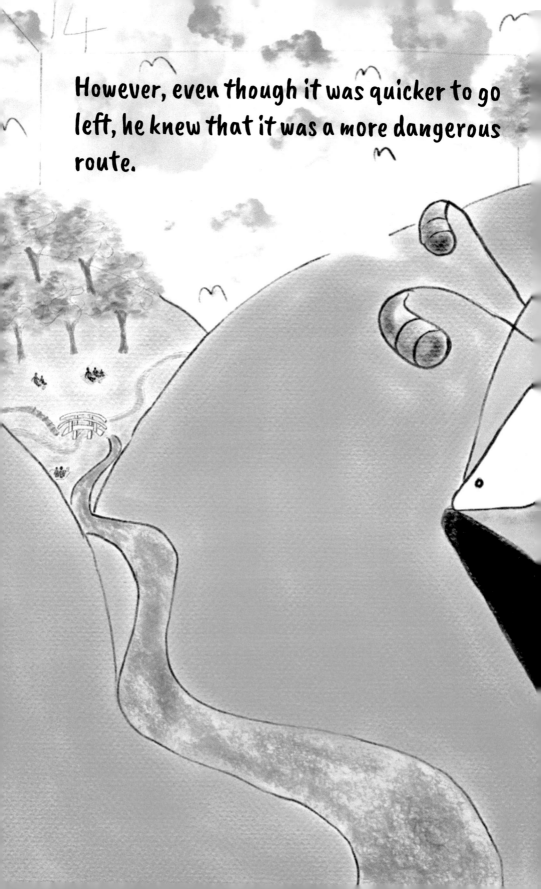

With his mind made up, Walliewasp took the left fork and he headed down towards Devil's Bridge.

In the summer months, Walliewasp knew that the strange-looking insects congregated at Devil's Bridge with their sweet drinks and delicious things to eat.

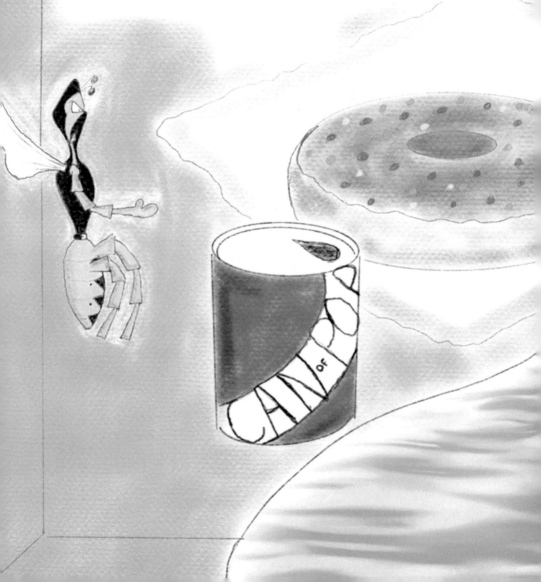

And one particular gathering seemed to have more than enough to eat and drink so Walliewasp landed on one of the delicious foods.

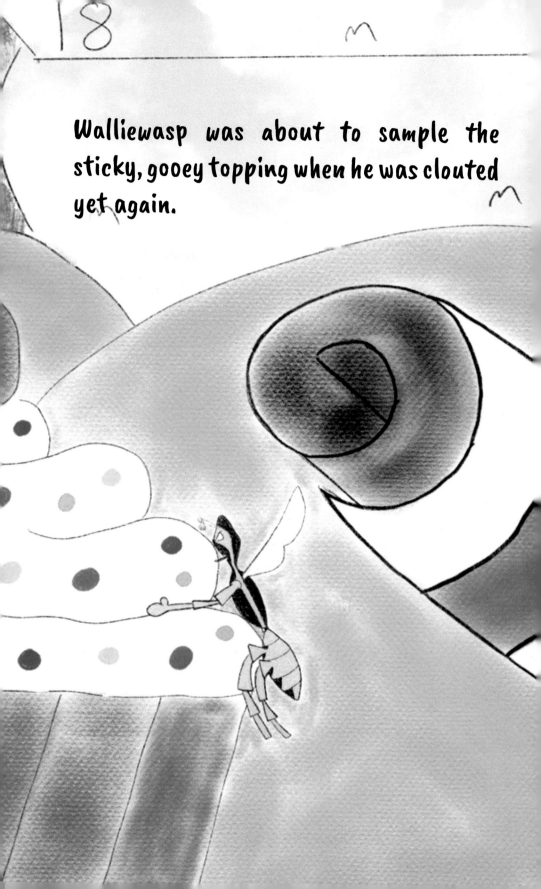

Walliewasp was about to sample the sticky, gooey topping when he was clouted yet again.

This time, he could feel himself hurtling towards the fast-moving river but he felt he couldn't stop himself from falling into the bubbling water.

Walliewasp was about to topple into the swift, swirling water when, all of a sudden, two grasping hands caught him by his belt and pulled him to safety.

As Walliewasp's senses slowly started to return to him, he realised who it was that had saved him.

It was his distant relative Benniebee, and the two of them sat on the riverbank catching their breath.

Walliewasp thanked his distant cousin Benniebee for saving him from the threatening water. And then it dawned on him...

Sometimes, one single act of kindness not only makes an insect's day, but it can also change their life forever.

With the thought of trying to be more understanding towards others, Walliewasp said goodbye to Benniebee and shifted his attention, once again, back to the mystical tree with its sumptuous fruit.

Walliewasp was not far from Swallows Wood now and he knew that once he was inside, he would be safe.

He would be safe because the semi-natural woodland would not allow any harm to befall any creature, great or small.

The valiant Walliewasp flew past the transition zone of the otherworldly wood and made his way to the special, mystical tree.

Walliewasp beheld the glorious, mystical tree and then he asked himself a very important question.

Is it possible for an ill-tempered insect like himself to change his stripes and become a more tolerant, open-minded living being? Walliewasp firmly believed that he could and with that, he darted towards the abundant fruit and tucked into the prize he had travelled so far to feast upon.

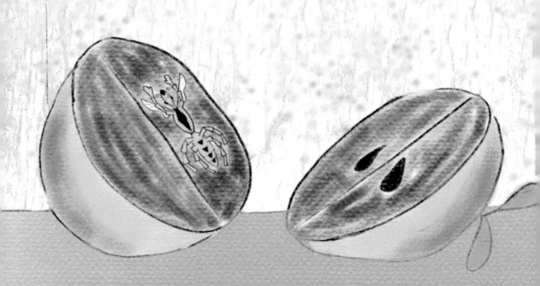